MW00974507

MAX AND KATIE'S
EGYPTIAN
ADVENTURE

BY SAMANTHA METCALF

ILLUSTRATED BY IAN R. WARD

Second edition
Published in Great Britain in 2018 by:
Mysteries in Time Limited
www.mysteriesintime.co.uk

Illustrated by Ian R. Ward.
www.ianrward.co.uk

A catalogue record for this book is available from the British Library.

ISBN 978-1-9997257-2-3

Hi! I'm Katie and I am 8 years old. Max is my older brother. He's really clever. He helps me with my homework when I'm stuck. He knows everything! But don't tell him I said that. He can get really annoying and be a real Mr Know-It-All. He is always telling me stuff, but sometimes it's just too much. All I want is a simple answer, like 'yes' or 'no'. Instead, it's always 'maybe, because...' So annoying.

But he's not so bad. He always looks out for me. And we have fun playing games together.

I think my favourite thing is playing outside in any weather! I love going to the park, especially the adventure playground with the huge, curly slide. You can go really fast on that one, especially when you lie down. Mum hates it when I come home covered in mud, but I can't help it. The fun parts of the park are always the muddiest.

Hey, I'm Max and I'm 11. I love reading. I read comics and cartoons that make me laugh, and I read adventure stories about knights and castles, or pirates and buried treasure! Mum is always telling me I have an over-active imagination. I can't help it. My mind just starts picturing loads of weird stuff.

I also love solving puzzles. Grandpa always buys me books full of word-searches and crosswords. I like to time myself and see how fast I can solve them.

Katie is my younger sister. She is really energetic and fun to be around. She's really fast and sporty. I wish I could be as good as her at sports. But don't tell her I said that. She can also be really annoying when she can't sit still for more than five minutes. And she doesn't stop talking!

But she's cool. I'm pleased she's my sister.

1

The sun was streaming through the window as Max jumped out of bed. He was excited because it was the last day of school before the long summer holidays. Mrs Elliot had promised her class that they would spend the last day of term playing games and solving tricky puzzles. Max loved solving puzzles. And he was very good at it. Not as good as Joe, his know-it-all classmate, but maybe today was the day when Max would finally beat him and come first. Max pictured the whole class cheering for him. He grinned at the image then bounded down the stairs.

In his excitement, he hadn't noticed Katie (his really annoying younger sister) jumping up and down at the foot of the stairs. He ran straight into her with a thump and they fell in a messy heap on the floor.

"What's wrong with you?" he grumbled. "Why

would you stand right there?"

Katie pushed Max away and jumped to her feet. "I couldn't wait! We have to open it together! Hurry UP!" she shouted.

"Open what?" Max replied, but Katie was already gone. He stood up, smoothed his hair and followed his impatient sister.

On the kitchen table there was a large, mysterious-looking box. He knew it wasn't his birthday. It definitely wasn't Christmas. So what could the parcel be? Max read the label. It was addressed to both of them. Together.

"Mum doesn't know who sent it or what's inside, but she made me wait for you to come down before I could open it," Katie moaned. "You took ages to get up. AGES!"

Together, they unwrapped the packaging and opened the box. Inside, they found a letter, also addressed to them. Max cleared his throat.

"You're sooo slow!" moaned Katie. "This century would be good!"

Max was good at ignoring his sister's grumpiness. He'd had lots of practice.

He read the letter out loud and Katie listened, her eyes huge with excitement.

Dear Max and Katie,

I need your help. I don't know who else to turn to.

But how can you help me? To explain everything properly, I must start at the beginning.

All throughout history, there have been millions of unsolved mysteries. There are people who lost something, lost someone, or were lost themselves. Nobody ever found out what happened and life was never the same again for these poor victims.

Imagine if you could travel back in time to help someone by solving mysteries that have puzzled experts for years.

A long time ago I invented a time machine, a way to return to exact moments in history. I have been travelling back in time as a detective helping thousands of people for many years.

Sadly, I am too old and weak to travel now. I need some help.

If you agree to help me, you will go on very special journeys, secret missions that you must never speak about to anyone. Ever. This is Top Secret. It would be a disaster if anyone else found out that time travel is real. People would use my machine for selfish reasons. That can never happen. I need to know that I can trust you.

I will not lie to you. It is not always easy. Some adventures may be dangerous.

Only read the Mission Plan if you agree to help, if you agree to keep this important secret. Think carefully. It is a big decision.

Good luck.

2

Max finished reading the letter. "That's weird," he said, frowning at the page. "There's no name at the bottom, no signature. We don't know who sent it."

"Does it matter?!" shrieked Katie. "People need our help. But more importantly, we're going on an adventure!"

Max watched his sister jump up and start dancing around the room with a huge smile on her face. She was right. Of course she was right! He started to smile to himself. An adventure *was* exciting.

They didn't have time to think about it now. "You'll be late for school! Hurry up you two," called Mum from downstairs.

They quickly put everything back inside the box and hid it in their Secret Hiding Place in the garden, where Mum could never find it. This was Top Secret.

Even from Mum.

They set off for school. Suddenly Max wasn't so excited about the classroom puzzles. He had real-life mysteries to solve.

Neither Max nor Katie could concentrate at all in school. Max didn't try to compete with Joe. He didn't even go near the Puzzle Corner. Mrs Elliot was confused. She knew Max had been looking forward to the last day's fun, so it made no sense that he was spending the afternoon staring through the window, watching the clouds drift by.

But Max didn't notice Mrs Elliot's concern. All he could think about was getting home quickly to get started.

This was going to be a memorable summer after all.

3

Max and Katie raced home from school and checked that the coast was clear. They took the box out of its hiding place and carried it up to Max's bedroom.

"Are you sure you want to do this?" asked Max.

"Hmmm. Let me think," replied Katie. "Do I want to have an amazing adventure that is Top Secret and fun and see things that nobody else gets to see while helping lots of people in history?" Her voice had got louder and louder.

"Shhhh! Ok, ok. When you put it like that… Well, here goes…"

Max opened the box. Inside, they found: a world map with a timeline; a timeline sticker; a sticker of a beetle; a booklet about Ancient Egypt; a hieroglyph chart to translate hieroglyphs; and a 'Mission Plan'.

They read the Mission Plan.

Mission Plan

Place: The town of Giza, Ancient Egypt
Date: 2540 BC

Just days after Pharaoh Nefarkamor died, his 9 year old daughter disappeared without a trace. Nobody knows what happened to her. Some believe she became a goddess, always watching over her father's body and riches. Stories were told about a lost girl trapped deep inside the pyramid. They said you could hear her crying inside the tomb for years after. But others said that was only a story to keep grave robbers away.

In 1998, archaeologists opened the tomb. It was sealed tight with no way in or out, so it had never been robbed. However, there was no treasure inside. It made no sense. Where were the riches that pharaohs were always buried with?

The mystery became stranger when the mummified remains were examined. The pharaoh had not died from old age.

Your Mission:

1.   Find some Ancient Egyptian clothes.
2.   Go back in time to the city of Giza in Ancient Egypt, 2540 BC.
3.   Find out who killed Pharaoh Nefarkamor, what happened to his daughter, and who stole his treasure.

Good luck.

4

Max and Katie knew just the place to find Egyptian clothes. "Mum, we're just going to visit Grandpa!" called Max.

"Don't be long," called Mum from the kitchen. "Dinner is nearly ready!"

Max and Katie looked at each other and grinned. Mum never had dinner ready when she said it would be. It always took much longer than she thought. They knew they had plenty of time.

They set off for their grandfather's fancy dress shop, which was just around the corner. On the way, they quickly got their story straight. They agreed to tell him that they were going to a fancy dress party and they wanted to dress up as Ancient Egyptians.

Inside the shop, their grandfather raised one eyebrow as Max went into too much detail and talked for too long, but he led them silently to the

back of the shop. He blew the dust off a rail of clothes and helped them choose the best costumes from an enormous selection.

Katie couldn't wait to try it on, but Max insisted they wait until they get home. He said he didn't want to get them dirty, but Katie knew he just didn't want to bump into anyone he knew on the way home while he was dressed as an Egyptian.

They thanked their smiling grandfather and headed home.

Back home, Max and Katie raced upstairs to avoid Mum. They couldn't face telling yet another lie. As soon as they were safely in Max's room, they closed the door and read the history book about Ancient Egypt from cover to cover, trying to learn and remember as much as possible. Well, Max read it from cover to cover. Katie just looked at the pictures and asked Max lots of annoying questions.

It was time to get dressed. Max wrapped a white linen sheet over his shoulders and around his waist like a white skirt. There was a colourful belt to tie it together at the waist.

Katie's dress wrapped around her, making a long skirt that reached the ground. She had wide straps over her shoulders and a bright blue belt.

They both had large colourful collars that covered their shoulders, and Katie had a matching headband with a green gem at the front.

They looked in the mirror together.

Max frowned at their reflection. He nudged his sister, who was busy striking a pose.

"Ouch!" she complained. "That hurt! And you're ruining my Ancient Egyptian pose. I look just like one of the ancient paintings!"

Max was impressed that she had listened to some of the Ancient Egypt facts after all.

"We don't want to draw attention to ourselves when we get there," he said. "We need to dress less like a pharaoh and more like everyone else."

Katie was standing with her arms folded, glaring at him. "You want to get rid of the collar and the headband, don't you?"

Katie already knew the answer. She also knew Max was right, but she wasn't going to admit that to him. Instead, she huffed as she took off the pretty items, giving them one last adoring glance before placing them on the bed.

Katie put the hieroglyph chart into her white, linen bag, just in case they needed it, then had another look in the mirror.

"Wow, we look just like the people in the history books!" laughed Katie. "But there's something missing…" She ran next door into the bathroom and returned with Mum's make-up bag.

"Oi! What are you doing?!" complained Max, as

his sister held a black pencil to his eye.

"Hold still!" she said. "Didn't you read the history book? All Ancient Egyptians used to wear black make-up around their eyes to keep the dazzling sun away." Katie smiled. "Even boys."

5

Max and Katie followed the strange instructions that came with the time machine.

First, they put the Time Travel Sticker on their clothes.

"What does this do?" asked Katie, turning her head on one side to look at the sticker better. It looked like a beetle with wings, playing with a football.

"This is like a tiny computer that translates everything we say into Ancient Egyptian," explained

Max, reading the instructions. "It's disguised to look like an amulet, so people won't notice it."

"Am-u-what?" she asked.

"An amulet was like a lucky charm that Ancient Egyptians wore to keep themselves safe from evil."

"Ooh, I like lucky charms! Especially one that makes me talk like an Egyptian!" replied Katie, admiring the design. "But why does it look like a flying beetle that's playing football?"

Max sighed. "It's a scarab beetle. And it's not a football," he explained. "It's the sun. The Ancient Egyptians believed the sun god Khepri rolled the sun across the sky every day, just like a scarab beetle rolled dung across the desert each day."

"Uurrghhh!" giggled Katie. "A dung beetle?!"

Max smiled too. It did seem funny.

They opened the map flat and smoothed it down with careful hands. They found modern-day Egypt on the map and added Ancient Egypt to the

timeline.

They turned the time machine on by pushing the switch on the side. Nothing happened. Confused, Max looked back at his instructions.

"It can be a bit slow to start sometimes," he read out loud. "Just give it a little tap on the side."

Max held his hand above the box, ready to tap it, when his impatient sister gave the machine a massive whack! Max threw his arms in the air. He opened and closed his mouth like a fish, speechless.

"What?!" she replied to his shocked stare. "You were taking too long!"

Max didn't have time to reply, because the machine had started to make a high-pitched buzzing sound. They programmed the time machine to take them to the city of Giza in the year 2540BC. They pulled the lever down. Their eyes were dazzled by a bright, colourful light as a current of electricity passed between the two rods on top.

"Wait!" shrieked Katie. "Do we know how to get back to modern day?"

"Good question," replied Max. His face disappeared behind the instructions as he looked for the answer.

"I don't want to get stuck in the past," Katie thought out loud. "Unless Ancient Egypt is a fun place to live and they worship us like gods and we live in the pharaoh's temple with servants and gold and jewels…"

Max interrupted his sister's rambling thoughts. "Don't worry. As soon as we solve the mystery, the tiny computer chip in the Time Travel Sticker will start working and we will be transported back straight away."

"Then let's hope we solve the mystery."

Max nodded. "Well, here goes!"

They held hands and took a deep breath as Max pushed the big, red button. After a few seconds, the four walls of Max's messy bedroom disappeared and they started to feel dizzy. It felt like they were on a roundabout in the park and one of the older children was spinning them really fast. Everything was changing all around them. Colours mixed together and everything became a blur.

Soon, colours started to form again as the world took shape around them. When their eyes had stopped spinning, they looked around. It had worked!

6

They were now in the middle of a busy market next to a large river, where people were carrying fish, bread and other food up the steps from simple boats.

Max was pleased that he was wearing thin, loose clothes, because the sun was hot and the air was dry. They both wrinkled their noses at the strong smell of fish and looked around at this unfamiliar place.

As Max and Katie looked for a way out of the busy market square, they heard two women talking.

"They are starting to embalm the body of poor Pharaoh Nefarkamor tomorrow, but the assistant has fallen ill," said an old lady with straight, black hair. "I hope the priest finds a replacement quickly."

Suddenly, behind them there was an enormous crash and they turned to see a large block of stone on its side, where it had fallen from the enormous wooden rollers. The men pulling it had all fallen over

21

and were brushing dust and sand out of their eyes.

A sharp scream pierced the air that sent chills up their spines. They quickly saw what had caused the scream. They could see the arm of a man stretching out from beneath the stone. Not moving. There was a birthmark in the shape of a strawberry on the unmoving wrist. The lifeless wrist.

"Let's get out of here," said Max. His face was suddenly very pale.

They climbed a small hill behind the market, wiping the sweat from their brows with the back of their hands. They found a quiet spot in the shade under a palm tree and sat down. In the distance they could see a half-built pyramid, with rows and rows of people pulling enormous blocks of stone along with thick rope.

"That looks like hard work," said Katie. "I think I even prefer school to that job."

7

"We need to find out what happened to the pharaoh's riches," said Max. "We need to get inside the pyramid before it is closed for more than 4000 years."

"But how?" asked Katie. "I'm sure it will be well guarded."

They both watched people moving around like ants in the distance. Then Max had an idea.

"Did you hear those ladies talking? The priest needs a new assistant," he said excitedly. "I need to get that job."

"Yes!" agreed Katie. "And I will try to get into the palace. There must be someone there who knows what will happen to the pharaoh's daughter," replied Katie. "Besides, I've always wanted to see inside a palace."

"Good idea, but be careful," warned Max. "I will

meet you back here before sunset." Max raced off to find the priest and offer his help.

After asking several people in the market, he eventually found the priest's house. It was at the end of a row of simple white houses that were all joined together.

There was an important-looking man sitting on a stone seat in the shade. Max guessed that this was the priest. He was talking to a tall lady who was carrying a bowl of fruit. As Max got closer, he saw the priest give a letter to the lady. The letter was rolled up with a thick red band wrapped around it.

They were talking very quietly so nobody else could hear and looked very serious.

After she left, Max was led into a garden for his interview, where he was quizzed about the method of mummification. He thought back to the history booklet and answered each question correctly.

However, the final question was strange.

8

"Did you meet the pharaoh when he was alive?"

"Er.. no, I am from a small village further south along the Nile," lied Max. "I never met him."

"Oh, excellent," said the priest. "Oh, er, I mean... pity. He was a great leader. You've got the job!"

Max thought this was odd, but had no time to think. Max followed a guard to a huge pyramid, where he was quickly distracted by how impressive the pyramid looked up close. They entered the cool, dark tomb. He was amazed at the thickness of the stones that formed the walls.

Max suddenly realised that the guard was now disappearing around a corner. He had to race to keep up with him. He didn't want to get left behind. Or lost.

They walked through a maze of cold, spooky corridors. The guard lit torches that were fixed to the wall along the way. The flames cast strange, flickering shadows that made Max feel nervous. His own shadow grew and grew until it filled the whole corridor, like a huge monster was following them.

They stopped in a large room with a wooden table in the middle. A man was lying on the table. A dead man.

Max stopped in his tracks. He had learnt all about the methods of mummification, but he hadn't prepared himself for the shock of seeing a real dead body.

He suddenly remembered a very spooky story about mummies coming to life and chasing people through dark corridors with their arms outstretched and bandages flying loose behind them. He shivered at the thought, gulped loudly, then decided to pretend the dead body was just a statue.

"It can't hurt you. It can't hurt you. It CAN'T!" he told himself.

Max was just starting to calm down, when a
huge shadow filled the room. He froze to the spot.
His wide eyes followed the sharp outline of a long,
animal snout, up to two pointed ears on the top of

the creature's head, down to the wide, powerful neck.

How was this monster so enormous? Max realised it had the body of a man and shrank back in fear.

Max had his back pressed flat against the cold stone wall. Just as his legs started to shake, the mysterious creature entered the tomb. Max blinked hard and looked again. Immediately, he felt silly. Why had he been so scared? It was the priest! It was just the torches making his shadow look enormous! The priest was wearing a mask in the shape of a jackal. Max remembered that this was the head of Anubis, the god of the dead.

It was time to mummify the pharaoh's body. The priest read some prayers and the body was prepared. The priest made a cut in the side of the body and removed the man's liver, intestines, stomach and lungs.

Although Max was ready with each canopic jar

for each organ, he kept his eyes fixed firmly in the opposite direction. He didn't need to see this man's insides to solve the mystery.

9

Meanwhile, Katie was in such a rush to get to the palace, that she ran straight into somebody with a crash. The tall, beautiful lady fell to the ground and dropped all the fruit she had been carrying. Dates and figs rolled off in different directions, but she didn't seem to care. She only seemed interested in picking up a rolled letter she had also dropped. Katie noticed it because the thick red band around its

middle was shiny and pretty.

"I'm so sorry!" said Katie. "I am so clumsy!"

Katie helped the lady up and ran after the runaway fruit.

"Not to worry, dear. No harm done," replied the lady kindly, after Katie had caught the last fig. "What's your name?"

"Katie," she replied. "Would you like me to help you carry your shopping into the palace?"

"Oh, that's very kind of you, dear. Thank you."

Katie smiled to herself. She had already found a way into the palace! Now all she needed was a little more luck so she could solve the whole mystery before Max even had a chance to beat her to it!

Inside the palace, Katie looked all around her, admiring the impressive building. She was amazed by the enormous statues that were carved from stone and decorated with dazzling gold. There were hieroglyphs carved into pillars and high ceilings up above.

Katie remembered she was there to do a job, and busied herself helping to put the fruit into a large bowl. She was just finishing when she saw a girl about her own age. She had short black hair with a colourful headdress. The girl was wearing a long, white dress, just like Katie, but she also had golden bracelets and rings with sparkling jewels of stunning blues and pretty greens.

"She's wearing such beautiful gems, so she must be the pharaoh's daughter," thought Katie. "She's the one who will disappear soon. I have to find a way to warn her."

But before she could do anything, the fruit lady walked up to the pharaoh's daughter and gave her the letter she had brought. The pharaoh's daughter read it, nodded to her in secret agreement and the lady left.

While Katie was thinking about how to approach

this girl, there was suddenly a terrible animal-like noise inside the palace. Katie realised it was coming from the girl. She was crying.

"It's horrible!" she wailed to a group of servants who were waving large palm leaves to keep her cool. "Why did the gods have to take him? What did he do to them?"

Katie stopped in her tracks. She recognised fake crying from a mile off. Katie was the Queen of Fake Crying at home. Whenever Max wanted to get his own way, all she had to do was scrunch up her eyes, hold her breath until her face turned red, and start sobbing at the top of her voice. Max would immediately get into trouble and she would win. She knew fake crying when she saw it.

But surely this girl must have real tears? Her father had just died.

Why would she need to fake cry?

10

Katie hid in the shadows and waited until the girl was alone. Sure enough, as soon as all the servants had left, the girl's face returned to normal very quickly. She even gave a little smile!

The girl checked there was nobody around and tiptoed to the middle of the stone wall. She pushed the wall with both hands and Katie could hardly believe her eyes – the wall moved!

It was a secret door! The girl had one more look around to check she was alone, then stepped into the shadows behind the door. The door closed behind her. It became a solid, flat wall again. Katie recovered from her surprise and tiptoed to the wall.

"Here goes!" she told herself. She took a deep breath and pushed the wall.

It worked! She almost clapped her hands in celebration, but stopped herself just in time.

Katie looked around, then silently followed the girl into the shadows. The door closed behind her.

She found herself inside a dark corridor with hieroglyphs painted on the wall. Now what? Which way had the pharaoh's daughter gone?

Katie peered in both directions. To the right, she saw a distant flicker of light. She felt her way along the walls in that direction, hoping not to bump into anything. Or anyone.

11

Back inside the pyramid, the priest was busy hammering a hole into the brain through the nose. Max nearly fainted at the loud crack as the chisel went through bone. Now it was time to remove the brain from the body. Max turned green. He knew what was coming.

"Don't be sick, don't be sick," he chanted silently to himself.

He held out the hook for the priest, but his hand was shaking so much that he knocked the dead man's arm. It fell down and Max's eyes were drawn to the inside wrist. There was a strawberry-shaped birthmark there. Where had he seen that before? Why was it important?

"Of course!" thought Max. He knew the answer. He didn't wait to see the priest push the long hook up through the nose. He didn't wait to hear the

squelch as the hook was swirled from side to side
and around. He didn't wait to see the mashed brain
flow from the nose. Instead, he bowed goodbye
to the priest and ran as fast as he could from the
pyramid into the fresh air.

He had to find Katie.

12

Katie found herself in a secret room. She heard hushed voices and tiptoed forward, hiding behind a tall pillar. She carefully peered around the edge, trying to ignore her thumping heart. The pharaoh's daughter was talking to someone, but Katie couldn't see who it was. They were hidden in shadows.

"We have received the letter from our trusted friend. We have to wait until dark," said the girl. "Then it will be time to go."

Who was she talking to? Why were they hiding inside a secret room?

Katie noticed a piece of thick paper on the floor by her feet. It was the letter! The girl must have dropped it. Katie picked it up and put it into her linen pouch to read later. She knew it was important.

Katie realised the girl was about to leave. She had to go now or she would be seen. Katie turned and

retraced her steps quietly. She found herself back where she had started.

"Oh no!" she whispered to herself. There were three doors to choose from. THREE! She hadn't noticed on her way in. She looked at the hieroglyphs on each door. "Which door will take me out of the palace?" Katie pulled out her hieroglyphs chart from her linen bag and started to translate the symbols.

"Why do some of the symbols look really

similar?!" she thought angrily.

She had to hurry. She could hear footsteps coming closer!

13

Katie translated the hieroglyphs just in time and emerged into the market through another secret door. She ran fast, hoping to find Max at their meeting place on the hill. Incredibly, Max arrived at exactly the same time. They were delighted to see each other and they quickly told each other everything that they had seen and heard. Katie showed her brother the piece of paper she had found.

"It's not paper, it's papyrus," explained Max. "It's what the Ancient Egyptians used to write on."

Katie rolled her eyes. She wasn't in the mood for one of Max's lessons.

"This is definitely the same note that the priest gave to the lady with the fruit," said Max. "This all makes sense now."

"Er, hello?" said Katie, waving her arm in front of

Max's face. "What makes sense?!"

Max ignored his sister. Instead, he studied the papyrus for a short time then stood up quickly. "It's nearly dark," he said, looking at the sky. "We need to go now. This note says there is a final meeting in the market at sunset."

Katie was confused. "What meeting?" she said, but he was already walking away quickly. "Hey – wait for me!" she shouted and ran after him. "Don't leave me here in the dark alone – the mummies will get me!"

14

Max and Katie ran down the hill to the market square. Everyone had gone home for dinner, so the market was deserted now. Well, it looked deserted at first, but Max soon realised that there were four other people there in the shadows. Katie and Max were heading straight for them. Clouds of dust and sand blew up around them as they skidded to a stop.

Katie shrieked in terror at the scary shapes around her. Her imagination started playing tricks on her. She saw a huge monster with a dog for a head, an evil goddess, as well as two mummies in ripped bandages hiding in the shadows, one the size of a child. Katie blinked hard and forced her eyes to adjust to the dark.

"Atchoo!" sneezed Max, as sand and dust settled in the air around them.

"Max?!" exclaimed the priest from the pyramid.

Of course it was the mask of Anubis, not a real monster! "What are you doing here?" he asked, removing his mask.

"Katie?!" said the nice lady from the palace. "Is that you?"

She wasn't an evil goddess after all!

Max and Katie were very relieved. They both looked closer. There were no mummies wrapped in bandages. They were really just a man and a girl, both wearing tatty, ripped clothes.

The young girl and the man looked terrified and started to back away.

"Don't be scared," said Max, realising what had happened. "We will keep your secret."

"What secret?" asked Katie, getting cross. She folded her arms across her body, scowling. "What is going on?"

15

Max explained. "The pharaoh didn't really die. He just pretended. The mummy inside the tomb is the poor man who got crushed by the huge stone in the market. I saw the birthmark on his arm inside the pyramid."

"But he must have been squashed like a pancake!" shrieked Katie. "How could he be mummified?"

"Yes, the stone did hit that poor man," explained

the man in the shadows. "But the stone was hollow underneath, so he wasn't fully crushed. He could be given a respectful burial."

"So where is the real pharaoh?" asked Katie.

Max pointed towards the man in the shadows. "This is the pharaoh and his daughter in disguise. They plan to disappear together. I just don't know why or where to."

The man with the blanket round his shoulders stepped forward. "Your brother is right. I am the pharaoh. But I am sick of this life. I feel like a prisoner. I cannot leave the palace on my own, I must always have soldiers with me and I must always wear such heavy robes," he explained.

Katie looked again and saw that Max was right. It really was the little girl from the palace!

"I want to live a simple life," he continued. "I want to have an orchard and grow my own fruit and vegetables. I have found a wonderful place next to the Nile. The soil is rich and I can be happy there," he said. He smiled at his daughter. "We can be happy there."

"It must be terrible being the richest people in Egypt," said Katie, her arms still folded.

Max shot his sister a warning look. "Ssshhhhh!" he hissed, nudging her with his elbow.

Max looked back at the pharaoh. "What about the riches that should be buried with you?" he asked. "I know that nothing was… er… will be buried inside the tomb."

The pharaoh's daughter explained that they had used some of the gold to buy the land. The rest they gave to the family of the man killed by the stone. "We were going to leave the tomb empty, but we knew grave robbers will eventually realise there is no mummy inside the pyramid. After that awful accident in the market, we saw our chance. They allowed us to bury his body inside the tomb in return for all the riches they could ever imagine! They were happy for him to be buried like a king."

"But I thought Egyptian kings got buried with lots of gold and jewels so they could live in the same luxury in the afterlife," said Max. "Didn't the family want that poor man to have a better afterlife?"

"He was poor in this life, but happy," answered the pharaoh. "They buried him with a single ruby amulet in his sarcophagus, but that was all. That would be enough for him to never be hungry, but not be changed by jealousy and greed."

"Being rich isn't what you think," said the pharaoh's daughter sadly. "You don't know who is nice to you just because you have money. I have never had a real friend, only servants who are told to play with me. I just want a real friend!"

Katie had a tear in her eye. Her arms were now by her sides. She realised that nothing is ever how it seems from the outside. She gave the young

Egyptian a hug and told her she will have lots of real friends soon.

Max and Katie wished them a happy life and waved them goodbye. They stepped back into the shadows just in time. Their adventure was over. The darkness slowly faded away and the familiar walls of Max's bedroom formed around them.

They were excited – they had solved the first mystery! They knew what had happened all those thousands of years ago. There had been no murder, no lost girl, no stolen treasure. There was only a happy father and daughter, choosing a different life for themselves. Some mysteries should stay mysteries.

They heard their mum calling from downstairs, "Dinner's ready!"

They both grinned.

Adventures make you hungry.

The End.

See you on our next adventure.

Also in the Mysteries in Time series:

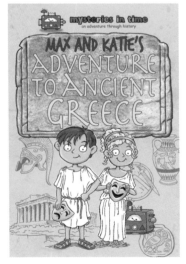

mysteries in time
an adventure through history

MAX AND KATIE'S

WILD WEST ADVENTURE

mysteries in time
an adventure through history

MAX AND KATIE'S

AZTEC ADVENTURE

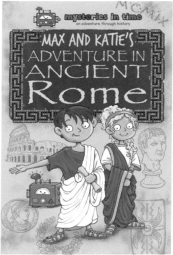

mysteries in time
an adventure through history

MAX AND KATIE'S

ADVENTURE IN ANCIENT Rome

mysteries in time
an adventure through history

MAX AND KATIE'S

VICTORIAN ADVENTURE

mysteries in time
an adventure through history

MAX AND KATIE'S
VIKING ADVENTURE

mysteries in time
an adventure through history

新年快乐

MAX AND KATIE'S
ADVENTURE IN ANCIENT CHINA

mysteries in time
an adventure through history

MAX AND KATIE'S
SPACE ADVENTURE

mysteries in time
an adventure through history

MAX AND KATIE'S
STUART ADVENTURE